Midnight Flame

by
Mary Wine

DRAGONBLADE PUBLISHING, INC.

ARE YOU SIGNED UP FOR DRAGONBLADE'S BLOG?

You'll get the latest news and information on exclusive giveaways, exclusive excerpts, coming releases, sales, free books, cover reveals and more.

Check out our complete list of authors, too!

No spam, no junk. That's a promise!

Sign Up Here

www.dragonbladepublishing.com

Dearest Reader;

Thank you for your support of a small press. At Dragonblade Publishing, we strive to bring you the highest quality Historical Romance from some of the best authors in the business. Without your support, there is no 'us', so we sincerely hope you adore these stories and find some new favorite authors along the way.

Happy Reading!

CEO, Dragonblade Publishing

Additional Dragonblade books by
Author Mary Wine

The Enchanted Well Series
Once Upon an Enchanted Well (Novella)

Highland Rogues Series
The Highlander's Demand (Book 1)
The Highlander's Destiny (Book 2)
The Highlander's Captive (Book 3)
The Highlander's Promise (Book 4)

Also from Mary Wine
Midnight Flame

Chapter One

THERE WERE MANY different sorts of bad luck.

There was poor luck, such as arriving at an inn on a snowy night to discover the last of the supper stew gone.

And there was bad luck. The sort of thing which everyone faced from time to time when life was in the mood to see you disappointed, no matter how much effort you invested in trying to obtain your goal.

And then, well then, there was the worst of the lot…cursed luck.

That thing which you simply were, and could not change, nor control.

"Come away from that looking glass now." Fiona was looking around the doorway opening to the loft where they both slept. "Your hair isn't going to be any less red for all the frowning you do."

"I know," Alanna replied.

"There's no need for all your worrying." Fiona was doing her best to be cheerful. "Your father adored you. It's far more than most of us have to get by on. Even though he's gone now, have faith that he left you a dowry."

"A dowry which will be controlled by his widow and her son." Alanna was back to frowning. She wanted to keep her spirits up, truly she did, for the only one to suffer from her melancholy mood would be herself.

Still, her father's widow loathed her.

That was no understatement. No dramatic elaboration.

Just simple truth.

Cursed fate...

"Well now." Fiona came all the way into the doorway. "The dowry will be known to others. You're illegitimate, but acknowledged. Those noble families are very good at finding matches for those girls with dowries. Now come away. It is a fine day, and the fair awaits. Do you wish your father's ghost to walk the earth because he sees you so forlorn?"

"No." Alanna forced her lips into a smile. Really, she needed to think of her father and the fact that he had in fact loved her. It was a blessing even if her stepmother deemed her a curse.

Alanna turned and smiled at Fiona. Her cousin beamed, and they headed down the steps, happily on their way to enjoy the harvest festival.

THE HARVEST WAS in.

It was a happy time, even though everyone knew the season of plenty was ending and winter looming. None of it mattered though as they took to the streets to enjoy a bountiful offering of fruit and bread. Musicians played happy tunes, ones which made everyone want to dance.

In the afternoon, there was a wedding. The bride wore a head wreath of braided wheat and barley, along with a bright smile.

But the sun set earlier, heralding the approach of shorter days, and the wind carried the bite of winter.

Tonight, the chill of the evening was banished as a huge fire was built up in one of the recently cleared fields. The children were sent off to their beds, as the younger adults danced around the flames beneath the dark night sky.

Alanna twirled around and around until her skirts rose up into the air. When she was too dizzy to continue, she collapsed into a heap and giggled at the night sky. Laying on her back, she gazed up at the stars, which managed to twinkle at her through the dark clouds that were growing more numerous.

The wind blew, and the dry stalks around her rustled. For all that she'd seen them during the day, illuminated by the firelight, and blown by the night wind, they took on a sinister nature that sent a little chill across her skin.

The night was a time of spirits and old magic.

Alanna lay for a long time, indulging her imagination as it made shadows into creatures with the help of the dying fire. Things were quiet now, the sounds of wind and fire dominate.

In the distance, there was the clopping of a horse's hooves. Alanna almost thought it to be just the mussing of her mind, but it grew louder.

Much too loud.

Alanna rolled over, realizing she was laying in the harvested field with dried barley stocks coming up to her shoulders. The fire was just a bed of embers, only glowing when the wind blew.

The man and horse were upon her as she rolled and rose out of the cut stocks which had concealed her.

The horse reared up, letting out a terrifying shriek.

Alanna stumbled back as someone screamed. Her own throat was sealed tight as she looked up to where the horse was snorting, its nostrils flaring out while its hooves pawed at the night.

And then it came crashing down, hitting the ground just a foot from her.

"Are ye daft?"

The master of the horse was a huge figure. He wore a black cloak which further concealed him in the ebony embrace of darkness. The stallion was the color of the night, too, making it nearly impossible to separate the rider from the stallion.

They were both glaring at her.

"Ye must be a simpleton to be laying in the field in the dead of night," he continued.

"I am hardly the only one here," Alanna answered.

He seemed surprised by her words, turning his head to look around. There were plenty of people looking toward him. The wind whipped up, causing the fire to glow red.

"The Beast himself…"

"Riding at midnight…because he's guided by ghosts…"

"Spawn of a sorceress…suckled on the icy cold breast of a witch…"

"Lucifer's henchman for certain…"

Alanna was close enough to see the man narrow his eyes as the whispers rose around them. There was suddenly a screech, and then a huge owl was swooping down. He lifted his arm, and the bird settled on his forearm.

"Time for you to run away…" he informed Alanna in a hard voice.

Considering how many people were in fact edging away, it might have been best for her to do as he said.

"I am not afeared of you, sir."

Alanna stood in place. Marveling at the sight of the owl and the man and the stallion so completely at ease in the darkness. Many men claimed to be courageous, yet this one proved the matter simply by being as he was.

The wind blew again. This time her unbound hair flared out around her. It caught the red glow of the embers as the moon managed to peek out from behind the clouds to illuminate her and the master of Stonebriar Tower.

There were gasps around them.

Alanna didn't pay them any mind. She raised her arm, not even sure when she decided to do it. The owl turned its head and then swooped down to perch on her forearm.

It was a surreal moment.

The thick wool of her sleeve shielded her from the creatures' talons, affording her the chance to simply marvel at the creature.

"Sweet merciful heavens...a handmaiden suited to Lucifer's henchman..."

The comment broke the magic of the moment, shattering Alanna's enjoyment as harsh reality gnashed at her. The owl raised its wings, flapping before it took flight as though it knew she no longer enjoyed having it on her forearm.

"It's just red hair..."

Her voice was thin and too full of need for her pride. The Master of Stonebriar peered intently at her for a moment; at least she felt that she had one soul who understood her misery.

It was a fleeting one. Gone almost as soon as she recognized it. He tightened his hands on the reins and dug his heels into the sides of the stallion to send the creature back into the night.

It left her standing alone. The wind blew, and she felt the icy touch of winter. She shivered as the horse's hooves dissipated into the darkness, leaving her wondering if the encounter had really happened or simply been a dream.

But the way everyone was staring at her was proof enough of the encounter. People whom she had danced with during the day now recoiled, some of them even making the sign of the cross over themselves.

She wanted to argue with them.

Craved the chance to make them see how foolish their fears were.

But no one would grant her that opportunity. The moment she locked gazes with anyone, that person would look away and then turn their back and head off.

A chill touched her nape, and it had naught to do with the changing season.

No, nothing at all to do with the weather.

Chapter Two

THERE WAS SOMETHING about nights after Samhain. Alanna woke in the middle of the night, staring into the blackness of her loft chamber.

They were colder of course. Alanna smiled at her own folly in noticing such a detail. It would be far more bitter when the snow fell.

It just seemed darker. Like the night was thicker and harder to see through. Tiny sounds somehow magnified into louder ones. She strained to hear whatever it was that had woken her.

A tapping.

On the window shutter.

Really, it is just the tree…

The single large tree which grew in the yard. She'd chased her cousin around its wide trunk when they were children. Tried to climb it when she was a youth. Now, its leaves were scattered on the ground, leaving the bare branches to tap on the closed window shutters like a boney, skeleton finger.

Enough…you are talking like the rest of the villagers now…

With a huff, she tossed her blankets back and got out of bed. The floorboards were cold, but she stomped toward the window shutters and undid the latch. When she opened one side, a gust of wind blew in. The sky was half full of clouds, allowing silver star shine to illuminate the yard.

The bare branches of the tree were dancing in the wind sure enough.

There...are you satisfied?

The wind blew, and a branch reached for her. Alanna gasped before frowning at her own emotional response.

Really...

She reached out and caught the branch. It was bare but it didn't snap easily. She had to fold it back and forth before it broke.

There had still been life in it.

Alanna felt remorse. The tree was a living thing. How could she make it suffer because her imagination was running wild?

The night wasn't so fearsome. She stepped closer to the open window. Everything was shimmering in silver light. The tree was just as thick as she recalled. On the ground, there was a blanket of fallen leaves. The wind gusted, and the leaves rose in arches making dry, rustling sounds.

Night music.

The bare branches added in their tap, tap, tap, and of course there was the wail of the wind. Music was a much better way to think of it. She closed her eyes and tried to hear the melody. The wind blew in on her, chilling her body, yet it seemed to fit the moment.

"There...see how she is making ready to ride out and commit witchery!"

"Drag her down before she can bedevil the children!"

Alanna's eyes popped open. The yard was brighter now, because several of the villagers had brought lanterns and even a couple of torches along with them.

No...it couldn't be...

True fear pierced her heart.

"Here now...what is this ruckus?" Henry appeared in the door of the barn. The senior man among the household, he slept in the loft.

"The Master of Stonebriar is riding again...we know he's looking for his handmaiden!"

"What handmaiden?" Henry inquired as he rubbed his eyes once more. "Go on with the lot of ye. The time for drinking yourselves half daft was last night."

There were too many of them for Henry to deal with. Behind the burly head of house, several lanky youths appeared.

"How can ye deny it when she stands there in naught but a smock…as warm as if in front of a fire?"

There was more gasping in response.

Alanna jumped back. The room that had always been her sanctuary was suddenly an inescapable prison. Panic was gripping her as she turned around several times, unable to decide what to do.

Someone pushed in the front door.

They did it so fast, it hit the wall.

Alanna grabbed her surcoat. The garment was hanging on a hook, ready for when she'd need it against winter's chill. She pushed her hands into the sleeves and ran toward where her boots were neatly stowed near the door.

They were coming up the stairs.

"What in heavens name are ye thinking to do?" Fiona's mother called out.

The door to Alanna's room burst inward.

"Get her…get her before she escapes!"

They caught her. Alanna screamed as they drug her toward the stairs and whatever fate they devised for her.

Chapter Three

"I SAID ENOUGH!" Henry had a solid looking club in his hands. He raised it up in warning as he stood in the doorway. "Get out of this house, and I won't speak of the matter again."

"The Master of Stonebriar has to be sated..."

"He's riding at night again...cursing the fields..."

"We'll starve..."

"Nonsense!" Henry bellowed. "Take yer tales of night doings to the tavern where they belong."

"Everyone saw the communion between them last night!"

There was a muttering of agreement.

"A bride will sate him...keep him away from our homes!"

Bride? Alanna blinked, shocked to hear they weren't planning some terrible thing.

You want to be taken to Stonebriar?

She definitely did not. However, it was a better fate than being tossed into the water to test her holiness.

"Aye...he needs a wife to settle his restless spirit! Everyone knows marriage is the cure for Rakehells!"

Henry raised the club up, but he was shoved aside as the group overwhelmed him. Alanna was carried out in their midst.

Like a fallen leaf being taken along by the current of a stream.

"Wait...ye cannae simply take the lass...what manner of people are ye?" Henry shouted from behind them. "She's but a wee lassie…Ye cannae take her to Stonebriar…."

His Scottish heritage came through because he was agitated. The borderlands were a place where Scot, Welsh, and English mingled freely.

It was also a place where legend and lore persisted, in spite of the Church's effort to eradicate the old pagan traditions.

And she was about to become one of those traditions.

They stopped only long enough to wrap her in a length of fine wool fabric. Around and around her it went, encasing her from shoulders to ankles. Making certain she couldn't move.

"Oh please…" Alanna wasn't precisely certain what she'd intended to say.

She wanted to live…

And somehow, she was going to find the way.

But she simply had no idea how to force her wishes into reality.

"HUSH NOW…THE TOWER is just beyond this rise…"

Beneath her, those carrying her were whispering.

"The Beast rode out…Ivy saw him…"

"Shh! He's the Master…there are certain to be minors in his lair!"

Hope flickered to life inside her. Alanna was so grateful for the relief from the tension which gripped her just as tightly as the fabric.

They were coming to their senses.

Of course they were. Passion could only flare for so long.

She'd be free soon…

Above her, the night sky had darkened. Clouds obscuring the stars. The wind was still whipping them. Her nose was near frozen now. Yet with her hands bound, she could not warm it. The wind blew again, and this time, she felt the scratch of ice.

"It's too early for snow...." someone whispered, their tone horrified.

"She is trying to stop us from delivering her to her Bridegroom...."

The snow started coming harder. Alanna blinked, but the tiny crystals clung to her eyelashes. In the air above her, it was being carried in streams. The small flakes growing into tufts like goose down.

"He'll be returning from his ride, let's leave her on the steps."

Alanna tried to argue. The wind carried her words away as though she'd never spoken.

It seemed only moments before she was lowered down and left to her fate.

The villagers didn't lock gazes with her. No, they didn't want to look at what they were doing. Yet to survive, they'd sacrifice her and drown themselves in drink to forget how evil a deed it was. They turned and scurried off.

Cowards...

Alanna didn't chastise herself for how harsh her thinking was.

No, they deserved it!

Not that her temper was going to be any help. She looked up, feeling another wave of panic go through her. Stretching up above her was a tower. It appeared black and dark and impossibly tall. The snow was being blown past it, almost parallel.

Like nature itself was different here.

Don't go letting your mind create demons....

It was fine advice. Especially since her mind offered up a crisp memory of the man who was the Master of Stonebriar. He'd had dark hair. But his gaze had been the thing she recalled most, for in that moment when she'd locked gazes with him, it had felt as though he could look straight into her soul.

Which was impossible of course....

Alanna shivered.

But she knew it wasn't due to the snow.

It was unnaturally silent, in that way it was when snow was falling. The quiet fit though, for she was alone there.

And completely at the mercy of whatever fate decided to do with her.

Chapter Four

A LANNA WAS STRAINING to hear something.
Anything...

As much as she wasn't looking forward to a meeting with the Master of Stonebriar, she would prefer it to freezing to death on the steps of his tower.

The villagers wouldn't be returning.

So that left her with only one prayer, and that was that he would return.

And soon.

Snow was already building up on top of the fabric wrapped around her body. With her head uncovered, the tiny ice crystals blew right into the strands of her hair to chill her scalp.

She listened intently again to the night. There was naught but the wind. It was still gusting. The snow coming in thick clumps.

She didn't want to die....

The worries she'd had just the day before seemed so trifling as she felt the snow chilling her head down even more. She was shivering now. Alanna flexed her toes to try and fend off numbness, but she knew her efforts would only prolong her suffering.

She continued.

Life was worth fighting for. Worth suffering for.

But her will wasn't equal to the wrath of the storm. She felt her warm breath on her lips as it left her body because the delicate surface of her lips was freezing.

Her body wasn't merely shaking now. The motion was harder, almost violent. Her teeth rattled.

It was a haunting sound, like the branch tapping on her window shutter.

A cold, desolate sound that belonged in graveyards.

She wanted to live!

Her eyes had closed at some point, and she forced them open, refusing to quit.

The owl was looking down on her.

"MASTER, LOOK…"

Alanna turned her head. The stallion was in the courtyard. Another man reached for its bridle as the Master of Stonebriar looked her way. The owl didn't make a sound, but the bird swooped between them, landing on the man's arm.

Another shudder contorted her body.

"Oh…oh…please…help…me…" She wanted the words to make it to him, but the wind was simply too fierce.

Yet it hurt to draw in breath. The insides of her very lungs were cringing at the frigid temperature of the air.

"Master, I believe she needs immediate assistance," the youth holding the bridle stated.

"Aye," the man spoke. "She does."

Truly, Alanna didn't know what she expected in the way of assistance, but having him scoop her up was surprising.

Who had such strength?

Clearly, the Master of Stonebriar did. For he pulled her from the ground and cradled her against his chest with ease, before heading up the steps and into the keep.

Her cheeks stung because the air was so warm inside.

Relief flowed through her as she continued to shake. He went through a passageway and up a set of steps. It was so dark, she couldn't decide where he was taking her. The only sound was a soft rasp of his breath and a howl from the wind beyond the open door.

Not that it mattered where he was taking her.

Shelter was shelter!

He laid her down at last, and she heard bed ropes squeak beneath her.

Her eyes widened.

Was she in a bed? With a man? She discovered herself grateful for how impossible it was to stop her teeth from chattering because she wanted to laugh at the absurdity of the moment.

"What a foolish...stupid thing to do," the man stated in a tone which under different circumstances, would have sliced her to the bone because it was so sharp.

For the moment, she was far too grateful to care.

"Thank...thank you," Alanna managed to say.

He growled.

For a moment, she thought the sound couldn't be real. But a glance at his face showed her his teeth were bared.

What had the villagers called him... *The Beast*...

"Just why females seem to think a way to snaring a man's heart is by appearing helpless...I truly do not comprehend."

He finally succeeded in finding the end of the piece of cloth. He yanked it hard, and she went rolling across the surface of the bed.

And right over the other side of it.

He snorted in response.

She watched his feet from beneath the bed as she tried to push herself up. But she was still shaking and moving quickly beyond her ability.

"You may dispense with the charade, Mistress," he snarled as he hooked her by the upper arms and hauled her unceremoniously off the floor. "I assure you, I am not in the least bit tempted by you. However numerous your charms appear to be."

Chapter Five

ALANNA WAS LESS than a step from him.

He still had his fingers wrapped around her upper arms.

Gratitude be damned!

Alanna flattened her hand on his chest and shoved with all of her might.

All he did was scoff at her efforts.

Her temper flared so hot, she wondered why it didn't chase the chill from her body. Alanna was certain she had never been so wrought in her entire life.

"The villagers seem to believe you are some sort of beast who needs to be appeased," she informed him tersely. "I have been torn from my bed and left here against my will."

His eyes narrowed in response to her tirade. One corner of his mouth actually twitched up into a mocking curve.

"As I said," he spoke without moving, "You have nothing to tempt me with, Mistress."

His words struck her hard. Sinking in deep and drawing blood.

Why?

Alanna had no answer for her question. And worse still, she felt unshed tears stinging her eyes. She couldn't bear the humiliation of having him see her eyes glistening. The only escape route available was over the bed. She flattened her hands on it, meaning to push herself off the floor with her feet and crawl to freedom.

There was a grunt from behind her. The sound was a mixture of disgust and being less than impressed by her actions.

A moment later, the bed ropes groaned as he rolled right over the surface of the bed to come up in front of her.

Defeated so very easily...

Alanna felt her eyes widen as she stared at him standing in between her and the door of the chamber. Fear clenched at her insides no matter how much she might have liked to resist it.

"Stay here, Mistress," he growled at her.

"I cannot remain here...with you...it is impossible," Alanna stammered as she pushed back onto her feet.

His expression tightened. "You should have considered your reputation before allowing yourself to be laid on the steps of my tower."

"I was brought here quite...helpless," Alanna insisted. But her tone was far from what she might have wished it to be. Instead of solid and confident, it came across her lips in a squeak, betraying how frayed her emotions were.

She had never been so near to hysteria in her life.

His expression softened. It was just a tiny easing of the lines around his mouth, and a flicker of something in his dark eyes that seemed to reassure her that he did not intend to harm her.

You are seeing what you wish to see...

Perhaps so.

Yet he appeared to be considering his next words before speaking.

"Whatever the circumstances under which you arrived," he said, "The storm beyond the walls of this tower do not care to hear them. The night is not fit for man nor beast. Otherwise, I would not have returned so early."

"Oh." Alanna looked toward one of the windows in the chamber. Its shutters were closed tightly, but there was still clearly a howling on the other side.

"You are here, madam, until fate decides otherwise."

COLD DID MAKE a person want to linger in a warm bed. Alanna stirred and realized that she had the bedding pulled all the way up and over her head. She had a corner of the thick comforter down across her eyes and even covering the tip of her nose.

She'd slept as soundly as a squirrel in its burrow.

Surely it was day.

She pushed the bedding back and shivered.

There was nothing for the chill in the air. A look across the chamber revealed a copper heater, but no one had placed coals in it. She went toward the window. Pulling the shutters open, she looked out. Everything was covered in fresh snow. Below her, there was nothing but white as far as she might see. The stable was across the yard, but there was no even a single set of tracks in the snow.

How could there be no one living at Stonebriar?

And why were they not awake?

Perhaps it was very early in the morning still.

A chill touched her nape which had nothing to do with the snow and everything to do with the strangeness of Stonebriar.

Well, best to get away while there was ample light.

She closed the window shutters and looked around. There didn't seem to be much light. Her belly rumbled long and loudly.

She reached toward the chamber door.

Would it be locked?

There was only one way to find out. Alanna grasped the handle. She gave it a tug, holding her breath as she waited to see if she was imprisoned.

The door opened.

She paused, looking back across the chamber. The length of fabric was laying on the floor. Alanna retrieved it to use against the chill on her way home. She hurried back across the floor but froze halfway to the door.

There was a chain laying across the floor by the wall.

She had to be seeing things…

The difficulty with not believing what her eyes showed her was that she went closer to the item in question.

It was definitely a chain.

Made of thick links, it was set into the solid stone of the wall with a spike. The chain was fairly long, ending in a shackle.

The room had been used to imprison someone. Maybe several someones.

She jumped back.

Well, it's not locked around you….get going!

Alanna needed no further urging.

Outside the doors, there was a small landing. Alanna peeked over the edge, sighting the steps that went around the side of the tower in a corkscrew. They were steep, making her marvel at the way she'd been carried up them last night.

He is as strong as a beast, best to get away at once…

That was sound advice.

She started down the steps, but the interior of the tower was so quiet, even her footfalls were heard.

Alanna froze.

She waited, but no other sound came in response. So, she began moving once more. As she went lower, she passed an arrow slit in the wall. She blinked, for it appeared that there was less light than when she'd looked out of the window in the chamber.

Had she truly slept the day away?

It seemed inconceivable, and yet, she feared she was correct.

Reaching the last step sent relief through her. At last, Alanna felt as though she might draw in a full breath. She stood for a moment, filling her lungs once, twice, and a third time.

You are not away…

She was not. Dawdling was ill advised to be sure.

Around her, the tower was quiet. She stepped away from the stairs, moving toward the doors. Anticipation sent her heart pounding. The twin halves of the doors were held closed with a simple bar of wood.

For certain, the Beast wouldn't worry about someone breaking in.

You're thinking like those mindless villagers now...he is just a man...

Well, Alanna would debate that he was a harder man than any she'd encountered before. But escape was her goal, and she needed to focus.

She pulled the bar free. Bending down, she laid it against one side of the door. Once she straightened up, she pulled on the other side.

It stuck.

Gripping the handle with both hands, Alanna pulled hard. She felt her muscles straining. It was a fight as she tried to pull harder, and yet, the door resisted her efforts.

Suddenly it broke free. She went stumbling backward. Alanna landed on her backside, looking at a frozen block of snow which went all the way to the top of the doorway.

Alanna blinked, having trouble absorbing what she saw.

How could there be so much snow here?

Of course, the wind had been gusting. So the snow was deeper on this side of the tower. She got to her feet, turning in a circle to look for another avenue of escape. But the only windows were a full story up.

You're stuck...

She didn't want to agree with herself.

So, she turned around and moved closer to the snow. Reaching out, she tested it with a fingertip.

Frozen solid.

Without a doubt, she was sealed inside.

With the Master of Stonebriar.

The Beast...

Chapter Six

SUDDENLY, FREEZING TO death was much more of a mercy than starving to death. For starving to death took much, much more time.

Stop thinking like a simpleton…

At last, her inner voice offered up something of use.

She truly did need to begin formulating useful thoughts. Or perhaps it was better to say she needed to plan.

But where to begin? How did she go about taking control of her circumstances?

The man had to have a name…

Alanna snapped her fingers and smiled as that idea came to her.

Very good!

If she knew his name, she wouldn't be given to thinking of him as the Beast.

Ha!

Her smile melted in response to her inner voice's sarcasm.

She wouldn't give into ridiculous fears when she had solid facts to guide her. Practicality was the wisest path to set her feet upon in life.

What little light there had been was fading. Somehow, the time it had taken her to come down from the chamber had been enough for the end of the day to arrive.

Her belly rumbled.

But that was nothing compared to the way her senses began to pick up every little sound as though it were loud enough to wake the dead.

The tower was so quiet.

Unnaturally so.

And then there was a crunch behind her.

In spite of her well thought out plans, Alanna gasped and went skidding away from the doors.

There was another crunch and gnashing. Like some bear was using its claws on the door. She heard the snow being pulled apart, the ice cracking, and at last, the sound of heavy breathing.

The last thing was a strong kick against the wooden panels of the door. No doubt designed to break the length of wood which had been across them. The panel flew inward as she covered her mouth to keep from squeaking.

"Is that you, Mistress?"

Even if she wanted to deny her fear, her thoughts still seemed to be frozen. A lanky young man looked in on her, his expression puzzled as she simply stared back at him.

Like a terrified maiden...

"I suppose you were trying to get out," the youth began. He reached up and tugged on his cap. "We thought to let it thaw out a bit. It was all frozen solid this morning."

He reached for something and then climbed over the mound of snow still remaining in front of the doors on his way inside. He had a huge basket, and the moment he got close, she smelled the food.

Her belly rumbled loudly.

"Oh...my apologies for not feeding you sooner, Mistress," the man said in a rush. "The Master's duty is done at night—"

"Miles!"

Alanna spun around so fast, she missed a step and felt her ankle bend. Pain shot up her leg, but she barely felt it as the Master of Stonebriar sent her a scathing look.

"She might be a spy."

SPY?

Now there was a horrible word.

Well, label.

Alanna opened her mouth to protest, but the Master of Stonebriar had reached her.

She hadn't imagined how strong he was, for the man towered a full foot above her own height. His shoulders seemed far wider than any man she had ever encountered. His man servant took the opportunity to scurry up the stairs while his Master was focused on her.

Alanna refused to cower. After all, she had nothing to be guilty over.

And it was time to make matters clear.

"I wouldn't be here if you didn't terrify the villagers so," Alanna informed him.

He smiled in response.

It wasn't at all a kind curving of his lips. No, the word to describe it was menacing. She drew in a stiff breath as he closed the distance between them. Alanna tipped her head back to keep their gazes locked.

And he didn't stop until he was far too close to her again.

"The villagers are wise to fear me," he rasped out. "I am everything to be feared, madam. You would do well to remember it."

She was trembling.

It was an instant response to him being so close. Her heart pounding inside of her chest and her lungs rising and falling in a rapid rate in order to keep pace. She felt the tremor running along all her limbs, and yet, there was something different about the feeling. Something which did not fit with the fear she'd felt in the past.

The need to stand firm in the face of his attempt to frighten her was stronger than any wisdom she possessed. Right then, Alanna was quite certain she'd spit in his eye if that was what it took to stand her ground.

He didn't miss it either. He closed that last step, clearly taking her challenge.

But she stood firm. "I am not frightened of you, sir."

"You are a foolhardy woman," he muttered.

He clasped her upper arms, the connection between them jolting her. She had never been so aware of another person before.

And she heard his breath rasp.

It seemed they shared the strange awareness of each other. That thought melted her fear clean away. Which left her tingling as anticipation flooded her.

But of what?

She searched his eyes, seeking the answer to her question. Something was flickering in those dark depths, something which beckoned her closer.

And he met her in the middle.

Tilting his head and pressing his mouth against hers in a kiss that stole her breath.

Chapter Seven

ALANNA HAD NEVER been kissed.

The sensation was jolting to say the least. In some corner of her mind, she was astounded by the sheer level of intensity of the moment. Her belly twisted and her nipples drew tight. All of it rushed through her like a spark. Red hot and seeming to come from nothing but a flint stone and an iron striker. Two cold items which when brought together, produced a spark which could illuminate the darkness and warm a frigid night.

He suddenly lifted his head, staring at her as though she'd done something to him. For the first time, she caught a hint of uncertainty in his dark eyes.

"Find someone else to be infatuated with," he growled at her.

"Infatuated?" Alanna was incredulous. "I am no such thing, I assure ye."

He turned on her, sweeping her from head to toe. "I remember very well the way you greeted me last evening with your hair flowing. I suppose you, like other girls your age, believe men cannot resist the sight of flowing hair."

He stepped closer again. Alanna discovered herself frozen in place, mesmerized by his approach. The strangest sensation was prickling across her skin. He reached out, grasping a lock of her hair. He raised it up, his gaze on it before his lips twisted into a mocking grin.

"So very sorry to disappoint you."

He was amused by her.

No...at her expense.

Alanna reached out and slapped his hand. The sound was loud in the silent tower.

"I can see the villagers were correct about one thing...you, sir, are indeed a Rakehell."

His eyes narrowed. Alana was surprised, somehow, she hadn't thought her barbed comment might actually strike him.

"You suffer from an ill temper," Alanna informed him.

His lips twitched and rose into what might be called a grin. "Were you thinking to secure yourself a good match in me? The family name might be an old one, but I have no interest in dancing on carpets in the court to amuse some royal heir in order to further my position."

"How many times must I tell you that I was taken against my will and brought here?"

He scoffed at her again. "You may repeat it as often as you like, yet a lie is a lie. Allowing me to kiss you has revealed your true intentions for being here."

Her temper flared. Controlling it seemed as impossible as willing the color of her hair to change. He'd stepped close to her once more, his lips curved into that mocking grin.

She reached out and slapped him. "Lecher. You disgrace your father's name. I will most happily leave this tower now that the path is open."

Alanna turned to make good on her words, but the beast behind her lifted his foot up and kicked the front door shut. It slammed, the sound so loud her ears rang.

"I am going..." she insisted.

"No, you are not."

Chapter Eight

THE MASTER OF Stonebriar reached out, cupping her shoulder. Alanna felt as though her heart stopped when he spun her around to face him once more.

He was furious with her.

Impulses were the path to ruin.

Alanna knew it well. For any outburst or rebellious act had always gained her a punishment.

Today would be no different.

The Beast's eyes glowed with his displeasure.

And a red outline of her hand had appeared on his cheek.

He reached out and clasped her wrist. The hold was hard but not bruising. A moment later, he tugged on her arm and leaned over. She stumbled toward him, and he hefted her right over his shoulder.

"Wait..."

He disregarded her completely, heading up the narrow steps with her over his shoulder like a freshly downed deer. The narrowness of the steps made her gasp. If she fell, she'd die for certain.

Alanna clasped him as the fear of tumbling off his shoulder gripped her.

He took her back to the chamber she'd been so happy to escape, crossing the floor and tossing her like a sack across the bed.

Only this time, he flattened his hands on either side of her head.

Looming over her, as the bed bounced, and the bed ropes creaked.

"What are you doing?" Honestly, she wanted to demand that question of him.

But her voice crossed her lips in a breathless, husky tone, which astounded her.

Was that truly her?

"I am leaning over you in bed," he answered her question quite precisely. But his tone was mocking once more.

He was toying with her...

Her cheeks burned hot with a blush. But instead of her temper flaring up, her emotions took a swing in the opposite direction. She drew in a shaky breath as two tears trickled down the sides of her face.

He recoiled.

"Why so stricken?" Alanna asked him honestly. "You seem to take such pains to behave so horribly...are you not pleased to see me broken before you?"

His forehead furrowed. "I have saved you from freezing to death on the steps of my home and roaming the tower as a discontented spirit."

"I was intent on making my way home today, sir," she informed him. "Yet you have returned me to this chamber."

Her tone was still betraying her by announcing how hurt she felt. As if injured feelings were ever useful for anything.

Alanna angrily wiped her face, doubling her determination to keep any more from falling. She fought to sit up.

"Do get out of my way."

He stood firmly in front of the chamber door.

"The sun is setting," he informed her.

"But...really...I could not have slept the day away..." She turned to look toward the window. Beneath its closed shutters, there wasn't even a hint of sunlight to offer her hope.

It was night.

And she'd be stuck here once more.

"You are fortunate to be alive, Mistress," he spoke again. "You might consider showing some gratitude. Had I not spent most of last night in here to keep you warm, I doubt you would be alive to worry so much about a mere kiss."

Her jaw dropped open.

It couldn't be so…

Alanna turned to look at the bed. She blinked as she tried to force herself to remember the dark hours of the past night. But what rose from her memory wasn't what she'd hoped for. As her face burned with another blush, she recalled the warmth of his body next to hers, and the feeling of his hands smoothing up and down her back.

There was a small sound of amusement from behind her. Alanna turned to look at him.

"Perhaps you will consider the kiss my due reward?" he asked mockingly.

"It was my first kiss…" Her thoughts were spilling straight out without any consideration. Otherwise, she never would have admitted such a thing to him.

The grin on his face melted away, leaving behind a serious look. Almost as though he didn't consider her argument to be unfounded.

As though he cared about trampling on her tender feelings…

"I accept your reprimand as my due," he announced in a raspy voice. "However, my conscience will not allow me to see you venturing out into the night when I know there is little chance of you surviving."

He was suddenly moving again. Closing the gap between them. She recoiled, but he was much faster than she was. Alanna gasped as he swept her off her feet, cradling her like she weighed nothing, and tossing her onto the bed once again.

Even before she finished bouncing, he had her ankle in his grasp. She heard the ominous rattle of the chain and then felt the shackle against the skin of her ankle.

The snap bounced around the chamber as horrifying as a scream.

Alanna sat up, reaching for her ankle. She pulled on the cold iron of the shackle, but it remained firmly locked in place.

"You...you...beast..." she hissed.

"You must remain inside, madam, for the sake of your own life," he spoke softly in response. "And I have not the men to set watch upon you while I perform my duty. This will have to suffice."

"I wondered why you had a shackle here, now I know what sort of monster you are." Her temper was building, and she cared not a bit if he considered it a fatal character flaw. If he reported her to the church, she was going to be delighted to confess just why she'd been driven to behaving like a shrew!

"I am guilty of what you charge me with," he admitted.

Alanna froze. His lips twitched in response to the horror on her face. He closed the distance between them, until he had his hands pressed on either side of her. She leaned back as that strange heat went rushing through her once more.

"Yet that does not mean I will allow you out into the woods on a night which I know is too cold for you." His voice was husky. "Perhaps I cannot bare to see your life squandered now that I have tasted your kiss."

His attention lowered to her lips. It was a moment that swelled up, seeming to last for an hour or even more. The delicate surface of her lips tingled, awakened somehow. Something glittered in his eyes. He leaned toward her, as if drawn by the same fever burning inside of her.

This time, his kiss was softer. He didn't press her mouth into submission but coaxed her into joining him. All of the impulses he seemed to awaken in her came forth. She mimicked the motions of his lips, tilting her head to the side so that their mouths could fuse more completely.

He lifted his mouth away, leaving her breathless.

"Forgive me, but my duty awaits."

Chapter Nine

ALANNA HEARD THE horses in the distance.

She recalled the stallion he rode very well. It was a truly fitting companion for the Master of Stonebriar. His men were shadows as well. She could only recall Miles's face, for the others had never looked directly at her.

She was off the bed and pulled the window shutters open as the chain rattled behind her.

Such an eerie sound...

Down in the courtyard, the lanky manservant had the stallion saddled. He held it firmly as the animal danced, clearly impatient to be away. The horse didn't have to wait very long. The Master of Stonebriar crossed through the virgin snow, leaving deep footprints in it on his way to the stallion.

Once he gained the saddle, she saw the snow clinging to his boots all the way past his knees.

He was correct about it being foolish to venture out into the night.

But that didn't please her. No, not a bit.

Below her, the men leaned forward and rode off into the night. The sound of the horses echoed through the courtyard until they vanished. Alanna was left listening to the howl of the wind.

So forlorn...

She shut the shutters, but the wind was still howling behind the sturdy wood.

Had he really claimed he was acting for her own good?

Alanna wanted to rage against the imprisonment, yet the memory of his kiss surfaced.

She'd kissed him back.

The impulse had been completely and fully followed though until he'd broken it off. Even the memory of it made her blush. She sighed.

But a scent came in with the next breath she drew. Her belly rumbled loudly in response. Looking around the chamber, Alanna spied the basket the manservant had carried. It was sitting on the small table near the chamber doorway.

The chain rattled when she took a step toward the basket. Whoever had installed the chain had measured its length well. Alanna was just able to reach the chair and table. She sat down and pushed a small length of wool fabric aside to see what the basket contained.

"Oh my…"

She didn't care if she was speaking to herself, for the contents of the basket were wonderous. There was a fresh round of bread and a thick chunk of cheese. A lovely apple was there along with a pottery bowl full of some dark stew. She picked up the bowl carefully, smiling when she found it still warm.

As she ate, her attention fell on the length of chain.

His duty…

She was very curious what it might be to include having a chamber that was set up as a prison for someone.

Well…not just anyone…

No. The chamber was quite nice. Even the shackle around her ankle was covered in soft leather. The bedding was fine and thick. There was even a comb on the table, along with two books. It was a place fit for a noble.

Duty…

The Master of Stonebriar was indeed a harsh man at times, but he didn't dress like a beast. No, his clothing had been well made and fashioned of good quality wool. Black dye was expensive as well.

The desire to know his name returned.

Honestly, you should be more concerned with how to get away…

She should. But there was something about the way fate was insisting she remain that made Alanna fear she would never again be free from Stonebriar. Just as surely as she was shackled, her life was somehow linked with that of the shadowy master of the tower.

What sent a shiver down her spine was the fact that she was not altogether horrified by that idea.

A FULL BELLY sent Alanna right back to sleep.

Perhaps her exposure to the storm had been more taxing than she'd realized.

This time, she dreamed.

Her mind was full of images of the way she'd shivered. Such bone-wracking tremors really shouldn't have been called shivers because they had been so much harsher.

The pain had penetrated deeper as well.

She shifted, turning in the bed, seeking warmth.

And she'd found it…

In slumber's grip, there was no way to ignore the memories of the way large, warm hands had stroked her back.

Or deny how much she'd enjoyed it.

Alanna jerked awake in the small hours of the night. It was the darkest and coldest time. The tower was eerily silent. She was more aware of it because of the way the wind howled outside, like it was trying to get inside.

The window shutters were rattling as they resisted the push of the wind. They were suddenly still as the main chamber doors cracked. Alanna looked toward them, trying to force her eyes to see in the blackness.

A faint glow was her reward. She blinked and realized that the light was coming from a small, tin lantern. She caught the scent of bee's wax and the smell of wet wool. Yet there was something else. Alanna drew in another breath to discern just what it might be.

Metallic...

Without a doubt, it was blood. She sat up.

"It would seem fate has decided that you be afforded the opportunity to repay your debt, Mistress."

The Master of Stonebriar stepped closer. As he moved, the light from the lantern washed over him, illuminating the bright red fluid glistening on the side of his shirt.

Someone had spilled his blood.

Chapter Ten

"**I** NEED YOU to stich this wound, Mistress."

Alanna was out of bed in an instant. "Sit down."

The amount of blood was worrisome. Yet his stride was still purposeful. He sat something down on the table and placed the lantern beside it.

A moment later, he pulled his shirt up and over his head.

The yellow light from the lantern was just enough to illuminate the sculpted ridges of his shoulders and chest. Alanna bit her lip as heat went coursing through her.

Behave...

Her inner voice was correct to admonish her. The scent of blood was thick, and the light glistened off it. She had a task to perform.

"What happened?" Alanna asked the question without recalling their rather odd circumstances.

She still didn't know his name...

"Duty is often dangerous, Mistress."

He did think you might be a spy...

Alanna looked through what he'd brought her. "I shall need hot water. Give me the key for this shackle."

"Make do with the whiskey."

There was a bottle among the supplies he'd brought with him. "It would be better for you to drink the whiskey. To dull the pain."

"And trust you?" he asked skeptically.

"As you said," Alanna responded firmly. "Fate has afforded me an opportunity to even out the dept I owe you."

"And you think I will trust you will not take the opportunity to take my horse and leave?"

There was a slice down his shoulder. Without her help, he would not be able to tend it.

"Your manservant seemed to be quite dedicated to your horse." Alanna pulled the waxed rope from the neck of the whiskey bottle. "I imagine he already has the creature unsaddled and in a nice warm stall."

"You imagine incorrectly."

"How so?" Alanna handed the whiskey to her patient.

He grasped the bottle and lifted it to his lips for a long drink. "It seems the spy I worried about overhearing my conversations was in fact a man I trusted. You can see how turning my back on him has turned out."

Alanna gasped. She looked at the clean slice. It was at an angle along his shoulder.

"Miles was aiming for your neck," she muttered in horror.

"Aye."

Alanna felt her temper flare up. This time, it was on behalf of the man sitting in front of her. She frowned in frustration as once again, she realized she did not know his name.

"Well, I will have this stitched up in a short time," Alanna muttered. "It will give us both a chance to learn more about one another. Our introduction certainly lacked a few details."

"You are the daughter of Sir John Saddler. May he rest in peace. Your mother was his mistress, and his widow despises the very sight of you. She sent you here to the border the moment her husband died. The villagers did in fact leave you on my steps. For that, I owe you my sincerest apologies. My duty is one best accomplished with an ugly reputation that keeps everyone well out of my path."

He paused to take another drink from the bottle. She smiled behind him, the apology warming her heart. Alanna moved the lantern closer so she might thread a needle.

"Have I missed anything?" he asked with a hint of smugness in his tone.

"It's your turn to introduce yourself to me." Alanna tried to make the stiches small and quick.

He returned the bottle to his lips.

She didn't press him. Instead, Alanna focused on her task. She knew she was hurting him, so best to be efficient. Even the strongest of men felt pain.

"Finished," Alanna declared as she tied off the last stich.

She heard the whiskey swish as he handed the bottle back to her.

"Douse it," he commanded.

Alanna watched the way his shoulders tightened as he braced himself. She gritted her teeth and poured some of the liquor directly onto the newly closed wound. Infection was the cause of far more deaths than wounds were.

His breath rasped.

The wind howled almost in the same moment.

The flame in the lantern danced.

He rose from the chair, turning to face her. It was strange the way the light from a candle seemed so vastly different than that of the sun. Just then, with the night enclosing them, it was as if that pool of light was their own personal fairy glen. A place of mystery and myth.

And unbridled impulses.

He was watching her. Studying her. Alanna discovered her breath frozen in her lungs as she waited to see what he would do.

He extended his hand, his palm facing up.

It was a polished gesture; one she answered without consideration, because it was so ingrained from her childhood lessons on deportment.

Alanna placed her hand into his and felt his finger close delicately around her own.

"I am Bastian Fulke," he introduced himself in a brassy rasp that sent a shiver down her spine.

His lips rose into the very first genuine smile she had ever seen on his face. Alanna discovered herself responding in kind as a warmth spread through her that was beyond her control.

It was pure response.

He lifted her hand to his lips, pressing a light kiss against the back of it before he released her. He stepped back, performing a polished reverence before he walked into the darkness and disappeared.

Bastian...

A name.

Alanna hugged her hand close to her heart as sensation swirled inside her as fierce and unbridled as the wind outside.

They might be even, but it seemed as though all that had accomplished was to end one chapter and leave her with the very clear understanding that there was a whole new chapter about to unfold.

And she was eager for it.

ALANNA AWOKE TO daylight.

She blinked and then smiled as she caught the brightness at the bottom of the closed window shutters.

But she frowned when she took her first steps, for the chain rattled.

One matter at a time...

At the moment, there was something to be happy about. She finished crossing to the window and opened the shutters. Bright sunlight spilled in through the glass. Alanna laughed, happiness flowing through her.

She leaned forward, nearly pressing the tip of her nose against the glass. The tower appeared to be up on a rise. All around there was a sparkling blanket of new snow. The small building nearest to the tower of Stonebriar was a small stable. Today she could see smoke rising from its chimney.

Her belly rumbled in response.

The smoke gave her hope that food was going to come her way. She turned around, intent on righting the bedding but froze.

There was a key sitting on the chair.

Bastian must have left it the night before.

And you were so besotted by his charm…you never noticed…

Her inner voice was correct. Alanna happily lifted it up. She put her foot on the seat of the chair so she might unlock the shackle. The key fit into the lock. It took a great deal of strength to turn it. For a moment, she feared it intended to stick. It gave with a click and grinding sound. Once the shackle was open, the weight of the chain drew it off the seat of the chair. It slithered down to the floor like a snake.

Good riddance.

She held onto the key for a long moment, for it represented something more than her freedom.

Trust.

A man such as Bastian did not place his faith in anyone easily.

She wanted to be worthy…

However, she had no idea just what was expected of her now.

Should she return home?

Three days ago, she would have answered yes instantly. Now though, Alanna discovered herself pondering the question.

Bastian has not bid you stay…

He had not. In fact, he'd left the key so she might be on her way.

Alanna sighed. Disappointment drew its claws across the very surface of her heart as she stood there knowing she'd come to the correct conclusion.

You haven't known him long enough to be saddened at leaving...

Once more, Alanna discovered herself thinking that but three days ago, she would have agreed with her inner voice.

Today was somehow vastly different though.

She was different.

At last, she understood all the warnings she'd received about being chaste before her wedding night. It would seem a single kiss had indeed broken through some barrier inside of her.

One perfect kiss...

Just thinking of it made her insides clench and her belly feel as though it was flipping over. There was an insane amount of sensation associated with recalling that moment when she'd been in Bastian's embrace.

Stop...

She had to listen to her logic. Yet doing so caused another wrench in her heart.

It made no sense.

None.

Alanna could not deny how she felt. No. The best she might do was push it all down inside of her so that no one would ever know how foolish she had been to fall under the spell of the Master of Stonebriar Tower.

Chapter Eleven

I T WAS TIME to go.

Alanna set her shoulders, determination sending her back toward the bed. She righted it before using a comb to smooth the strands of her hair. At last, she was ready to venture back to her home.

Her last task was to gather up the remains of the basket of food. She stacked the dishes inside the basket and set the key to the shackle on the table.

But something caught her eye on the floor beneath the table. Stooping down, she reached out to retrieve it.

The letter must have fallen out of Bastian's clothing.

The parchment was fine and so very smooth against her fingertips. Only her father's wife used such a fine paper for her letters.

A little chill went down her back.

The memory of the wound on Bastian's shoulder rose from her memory as she was poised to turn the letter over.

There would be a name on the front of it.

At least, that was likely.

Spy...

She didn't want to be labeled one. Alanna stood quickly and reached into the basket for the linen cover cloth. She wrapped it around the letter, ensuring that she wouldn't see any writing on the front of it.

Satisfaction went through her as she blew out a long breath. It was strange the way temptation was so very hard to resist.

Yet she'd prevailed.

She turned around and jumped. Bastian was standing in the doorway, watching her with his brows lowered.

"I believe this is yours..." she muttered as she extended the letter toward him.

He took it from her fingers.

"Why did you wrap it?" Bastian inquired.

"It seemed...prudent," Alanna replied. "Since your duty is one which has you concerned with spies, I rather thought it best not to see the front of it."

His expression remained dark. "If you had turned it over, I would have had to keep you here."

Something glittered in his eyes which looked a bit like disappointment.

"Would you prefer I had done so?" It was beyond bold of her to ask such a thing. Yet she couldn't seem to stop herself.

His expression changed.

Warming...

Bastian tucked the letter into his doublet and came toward her.

He was going to kiss her.

Alanna knew it. Could see the intent glittering in his dark eyes. An answering need was simmering away inside of her. She stood in place, feeling anticipation tingling along her limbs as he closed the last pace between them.

She hadn't realized how much she'd longed for his embrace...

The moment his arms wrapped around her, Alanna felt a surge of satisfaction. It was a flood really, one which she gave herself over to freely.

No...wantonly...

This kiss was unlike the one before. That had been the first kiss between them. Now, Alanna was hungry, and so was Bastian.

He pressed her to open her mouth, kissing her deeper, and she happily met him. It was as if she'd awoken. All of the years of her life which went before were ones where she had been drowsy and half aware of the depths of feeling her body was capable of.

Bastian cradled her neck in one hand. It was a controlling grip, yet Alanna discovered there was something deeply satisfying in knowing he wanted to bind her to him.

It was proof of his desire.

She reached for him, needing to prove her own feelings to him. Her fingertips had become sensitive. Beneath them, she found the hard ridges of his chest a pure delight to trace across.

Heat was building inside her. Her clothing became too hot, and his clothing frustrated her. She tugged on the ties which held the collar of his shirt closed.

Bastian suddenly stopped. Lifting his mouth from hers and leaving her gasping. Their gazes locked, allowing her to see the hunger flickering in his eyes.

"I must return you home or accept I am truly the Beast the villagers call me."

Chapter Twelve

GOOD SENSE.

Just a few short days ago, Alanna would have described herself as a person of level-headed thinking.

Now?

Well now, she looked around the loft bedroom at her aunt's house and sighed.

"Come now," Fiona was quick to speak. "Do not sound so forlorn. I am ever so grateful you have returned home, Alanna."

"I missed you as well," Alanna responded.

Fiona fixed her with an unconvinced look. "Yet you long for the Master of Stonebriar."

Alanna could hardly deny it. "He is a man of honor."

Her cousin was surprised. Alanna nodded firmly.

"I do not know the details of his duty, yet I know he had ample opportunity to take advantage of me and yet, he did not," Alanna confessed. "If he possessed an evil soul, he would have acted upon his baser urges. A dog can't ignore a feast laid out before it. Only a man of morals can govern his own nature. I am a maiden still."

And she'd declare it to anyone who thought to blacken Bastian's honor by saying otherwise.

"Tell me," Fiona lowered her voice, "Did he...make your insides quiver?"

"Fiona," Alanna admonished her cousin.

Fiona frowned and opened her arms up wide. "No one else is about. My mother is doing her best to have me wed in spring…are you going to send me to my bridegroom without a hint of what to expect beyond my mother's lectures of wives being obedient?"

"I can hardly explain what I do not understand myself," Alanna replied.

Her cousin's features softened. "Did he…was he…beastly?"

Alanna was lost for a moment in memory. But Fiona gasped in response to the expression that appeared on Alanna's face.

"You must not think ill of Bastian," Alanna insisted. "If he had not cared for me, I would have died. The villagers left me in the storm."

Fiona's eyes narrowed. "Henry went down to the market the next day and pointed every one of them out to the clergy. I don't much agree with them only receiving time in the stocks. They tore you from your bed and now…"

Fiona suddenly bit her lip. Her eyes had widened, proving she'd failed to keep some secret from spilling.

"Now…what?" Alanna pressed.

"Oh…you will know anyway." Fiona lifted her shoulders in a shrug. "My mother wrote to your father's heir and widow. She thought it the correct thing to do, only now I understand the Lady Wydeville herself is on her way here."

Alanna really could not have expected anything else. It would seem that her fate was still an unkind one.

Cursed luck…

The villagers might have suffered the stocks for their actions, but Alanna would have to pay as well.

And the price would be her reputation.

THE NIGHT HOURS had become her sanctuary.

Alanna discovered herself awake in the dark hours of the early morning.

You are looking for Bastian...

She did not deny it.

She longed for him. Sinful or not, passion lingered in her. At night, it seemed to be the most intense. That thought made her smile, for the night suited the Master of Stonebriar.

The chill in the air was much more welcome with the heat of passion burning in her blood. She wanted to open the window but didn't dare. The look on the villagers' faces when they had spied her in the window still haunted her.

The night was not evil.

Or if it was...she truly was a handmaiden fit for the man who rode through it.

BASTIAN KNEW WHERE Alanna slept.

He watched the way the moonlight illuminated the closed shutters over her loft window.

He longed for her.

There were always times when duty prevented him from following his impulses. Alanna was something different though. She was far more than something he wanted to quench his desire for.

He barely knew her, and yet, for the second time in a week he was back, watching her window shutters.

They remained closed.

Clearly, she was wiser than he was. She was tucked into her maiden's bed, refusing to answer the call of darker urgings.

She'd kissed him back...

He recalled it clearly. Felt his cock hardening at the recollection of the way she'd stroked his chest.

But his duty was not yet completed.

Bastian tightened his grip on himself, forcing himself to turn around and leave Alanna behind. He had pledged his service to England. For now, that meant the night was his battlefield.

Alanna didn't belong in the darkness.

THE DAYS HAD grown shorter.

Alanna struggled to finish the washing before the sun dipped down on the horizon.

At least the wind helped dry it all.

It was dusk as she managed to haul the last basket up to the manor house. The chickens were agitated, so she left the basket and headed around behind the long building which served as a stable. The hens were on the far side to protect them from the winter winds. Several of the birds cried out in fright.

A fox no doubt. Looking for an easy supper.

She hurried around the building. "Away, away with you!"

But there was no fox.

Alanna stared at the hens. They were sill agitated and moving in jerky little motions around their nests. She ventured closer, noticing several large rocks sitting on the top of the stone nest boxes.

"What—"

She never finished asking her question. Pain exploded in her head as someone hit her from behind. Blackness came up like a giant cloak, wrapping around her and smothering her consciousness.

Chapter Thirteen

B ASTIAN DIDN'T QUITE believe his eyes.
         As his horse covered the distance to Stonebriar, he squinted. There was a figure standing on the front steps. It was very clearly a woman.

Or a lad wearing skirts.

He couldn't afford to lower his guard. The stiches in his shoulder were a fine reminder of what happened when he trusted the wrong person.

"Bastian..." the voice that came through the darkness was clearly that of a woman.

But it wasn't Alanna.

Bastian leaned forward, kneeing his stallion faster. A knot was forming in his gut as he got close enough to recognize Alanna's cousin.

"I am Fiona, Alanna's—"

"I am aware of who you are." Bastian dismounted in front of her. "Why are you here Mistress Fiona?"

The sun had yet to rise. Fiona surprised him by taking a deep breath and gathering her courage. She held out a letter.

"Someone took Alanna away," Fiona spoke as Bastian took the letter. "I found this in the chicken yard next to a rock with blood on it."

Bastian read the letter twice. He looked at Fiona. "I am appreciative of your efforts to bring this here, Mistress. Very appreciative."

"Alanna said you are a man of honor," Fiona replied firmly.

"Even if I am, the night is not a fit place for you to be alone," Bastian admonished her.

Fiona shook her head. "I would walk across Purgatory if that was what was needed to get my cousin help. I hope you are every bit of the east the villagers claim you are. Whoever has taken my cousin deserves to face nothing less."

"I promise you, Mistress, whoever has dared to put their hands on Alanna will have no mercy." He bared his teeth. "Not a single shred."

HER HEAD WAS throbbing.

Alanna imagined that was a good sign. After all, she wouldn't hurt if she were dead.

But the ache was truly dreadful.

She felt like she was being turned around and around in a circle. Her belly was queasy. She struggled to open her eyes. Darkness was all she saw.

She was bound to a tree. Her arms were stretched out behind her, and her wrists secured like some backward hug.

The bark was rough against her back, making her regret that she'd worn a lighter-weight dress. Now she was chilled. There was still snow on the ground, but in front of her, it was marred by the footsteps of whoever had abducted her.

Were they close by?

She looked side to side, gasping when she saw him.

"I suppose I should apologize for hitting you, Mistress," Miles spoke softly. "There is no point in doing so though, for I am not yet finished offending you."

Fear jolted through her. Miles fingered the point of a wicked looking dagger. The clouds shifted, allowing the moonlight to illuminate him.

The smile on his face was grotesque.

Miles snickered softly in response to her gasp of horror. He held up the dagger, moving it closer to her neck.

Her heart was beating at a frantic pace. Fear was trying to take control of her as Miles drew the blade across the skin of her neck.

"I do believe Bastian likes you..." Miles cooed next to her ear. "Surprising really, for I rather thought him heartless. I suppose we shall see if he arrives to rescue you. That's how to prove the matter...isn't it now?"

A new fear clenched its icy grip around her heart. Only this was a fear for Bastian. It melted away any thought she had for herself, leaving her focused on protecting Bastian.

Miles was a spy.

Never in her life had she thought to have dealings with such people, nor did she understand fully what the matter was that Bastian considered himself duty bound to protecting.

Whatever it was, Miles had attempted murder in order to claim victory.

All that mattered at the moment was to keep herself from being used against Bastian.

"He dropped me back at my aunt's home," Alanna began. She stopped and cautioned herself to speak slowly as she pulled on whatever it was binding her wrists behind the tree. "He has no interest in me at all."

Miles was silent for a moment.

Alanna realized it was a strip of cloth holding her prisoner. Likely torn from her own under slip. The lighter weight dress was suddenly her salvation, for the fabric was not as sturdy as her other dresses.

She began to rub it on the bark.

"What do you seek?" she asked to cover the sound of her motions.

"Perhaps I know the answer."

"I served Bastian Fulke for almost a year," Miles growled in clear frustration. "He never allowed the name of his lord to slip across his lips. You will have had no better luck."

Alanna bit her lip as she scraped her hands. Abrading her skin was of no consequence.

"I suppose you sliced Bastian in the hope of claiming that letter for yourself," she muttered.

Miles sucked a breath in. "What do you know about the letter?"

Miles was suddenly there with the tip of his dagger at her throat.

She needed time.

"Oh…oh no…don't hurt me…." Alanna tried to put as much emotion into her cry as she might. She gasped and forced herself to go limp. It was one of the most challenging things she had ever done. The point of the dagger made her want to rise onto her toes to escape its sharp point.

Instead, she slumped, ordering her knees to bend so she might crumple.

Miles snorted with disgust.

"Stupid weakling female."

Alanna heard him pacing. The snow crunched beneath his angry footfalls. The tip of the dagger had cut a line along her neck. It stung, and she caught the scent of her own blood.

Be still…

Time was what Bastian needed.

And if he does not come?

Then she would be dead. But she was content with that knowledge, for Alanna suddenly realized that if Bastian didn't value her enough to come, she didn't want to live the rest of her life knowing she loved him in vain.

Chapter Fourteen

"H E WOULD NEVER have told her."

Another man was there in the dark.

"Bastian wouldn't be the first to lose his secrets to a pretty wench," Miles insisted. "Go get some water from the river to wake her up with."

"I doubt it will do any good. You hit her too hard."

Despite his argument, Alanna heard crunching snow as the man started to walk away to do as he was told.

She pulled on the binding, desperate to make use of the moment to escape. But she remained bound to the tree. The strip of cloth dug into her wrists, sending agony up her arms.

Alanna kept pulling.

Suddenly, the strip snapped. Her arms flopped forward because of how hard she'd been pulling. She froze, listening intently to the sounds around her.

There was a crunch, telling her where Miles was.

Alanna opened her eyes, looking for him. He was several feet away, peering intently into the woods. She heard him snort, clearly frustrated before he stepped away into the trees.

At last, good luck...

If it turned out that her entire life of bad luck was being repaid in that single moment, Alanna decided she was content. So long as she was not the bait in the trap which Bastian died in. She pushed off the snow and stood.

The sound of Miles's footsteps was still going away from her.

She turned and looked behind her. In the darkness, the trees stretched their leafless branches skyward. Alanna looked up at the sky. The clouds were moving across the face of the quarter moon. Everything went dark as a result.

'Thank you...'

She forced herself to move slowly, so the snow wouldn't crunch as loudly. Still, every footfall made her cringe. Her heart was beating madly, so much so, that sweat dampened her hairline.

But which way to go?

She didn't know. A mistake would be disastrous. She looked up, focusing on the snow.

She needed to conceal her tracks...

There was a shimmer. Alanna blinked, uncertain of what she'd seen. The blood was roaring in her ears, or perhaps it was the water of the river. She simply didn't know.

But the shimmer was there. Off to her right. As the clouds shifted, she was startled to see her father. He lifted his hand, beckoning her toward him.

Was the spirit real?

Or just an enchantment formed from her fear?

Alanna didn't have time to debate the issue. She pushed off the trunk of the tree she was leaning on.

Her father smiled with approval.

And then he was gone.

But in front of her was a section of ground which had only patches of snow because the trees were so dense above it.

Thank you, Father.

Alanna felt hope blossoming to life inside her. She hiked her skirts and ran. The footing was rough. Every step was a flirtation with tumbling, but she continued on.

"You bitch!" Miles shouted from behind her. "I am going to make you pay."

She heard him give chase. His footfalls hard and closing. Alanna pressed herself to go faster. But he reached out and cupped her shoulder.

She let out a scream, terror finally winning control over her.

Miles growled with victory, his fingertips biting into her flesh. Alanna dug her feet into the damp ground, smelling the scent of decaying leaves. She twisted away from the grip, tearing herself out of it by diving forward.

Freedom was her reward, but she went rolling head over heels. She covered several feet before she stopped, flat on her back.

Something cried overhead.

Alanna looked up, seeing Miles standing over her.

"I'm going to slice your tendons so you cannot do that again..." Pure evil coated his words. Without a doubt, he intended to make good on his threat. Miles drew his dagger, angling it back and forth to show off the blade.

Alanna pushed against the ground, clawing at it with her fingers. All she managed was to scoot back a few inches. Precious inches, but Miles snickered at her efforts.

"Did you give yourself to Bastian?" Miles asked. "He's helping our bastard king to lead this country away from the true faith."

The cry came again.

This time, she saw the owl as it swooped low between her and Miles, its wings stretched out wide.

"No..." Miles hissed. His eyes bulged. His expression frozen as his mouth opened wide.

The expression on his face was death. Of knowing he was dying, while still alive. The clouds shifted, and moonlight shone down on the point of another dagger protruding through Miles's chest.

Its tip shimmered with blood.

Miles jerked. Relief hit her as though it had struck her like a bolt of lightning. Bastian's face came into view as Alanna relaxed.

But Miles' eyes shifted. He suddenly drove his own dagger backward. Bastian's face contorted in pain. Alanna curled her body up as she pushed her hands down flat on the ground beside her hips to help herself rise faster.

The ground beneath her was suddenly falling.

And she was going with it.

Straight into the river.

Chapter Fifteen

ALANNA LANDED IN the water.

As she fell, she caught a glimpse of the edges of the bank that stuck out over the riverbed. In spring, when the water had been high, it had eaten away at those banks.

Her luck was still cursed.

She splashed into the river. Sinking below the surface instantly.

It hurt...

The water was so cold! She cried out as it wrapped around her, chilling her to the bone. The current caught her skirt, using it to tug her down.

There was so much pain. She wanted to fight. And yet, Bastian's face flashed through her mind. Miles had stabbed him.

Wasn't that war though?

No one ever really won.

It was just an ongoing fight.

The water yanked her down. Her head went right under the surface again. Alanna fought. But in the darkness, she was tumbling, and remembering which way was up seemed to be hard. Her thoughts were moving slowly. Like a comb through tangled hair.

You shall not give up...

Alanna obeyed her inner voice. She renewed her fight to gain the surface. Her reward was a huge gasp of air that sated the burning in her lungs. Satisfaction went through her as she blinked the water from her eyes. Ahead of her, the branches were curled toward the water like a hundred boney fingers reaching for her. The sound of the river roared in her ears.

Don't...don't...let your reason deteriorate...

Alanna wanted to be stronger than her fear. But it was feeding on a thousand winter nights spent listening to stories about ghosts and the terrors which lived in the veil of the darkest nights.

She was going to know the truth soon...

The current was pulling harder on her skirts. Without a doubt, Alanna knew she wouldn't surface again.

Her strength was spent.

Perhaps she'd become a maiden ghost of the forest...the rest of her unfortunate sisters would welcome her....to an eternity of restlessness...

Alanna was suddenly jerked from the grip of the current. She cried out, feeling as though her arm was being torn from her shoulder. She flopped and flailed as she was pulled from the water.

"I have you..." Bastian's voice was sweeter than anything she had ever heard.

Her thoughts were still moving so slowly. Alanna tried to move her head. Wanted so very much to see Bastian's face. When their gazes fused, she smiled.

She smelled the blood on him...

It wasn't the restless maidens of the night who had come for her, it was her lover.

"I have you Alanna," Bastian's voice was raspy. "I shall never let you go again."

"Now that we are dead...we can be together...that is very nice..." Alanna muttered against his chest.

Alanna reached up to touch him. He caught her hand in his.

"You are warm," Alanna exclaimed. "You are not dead."

Her mind simply wasn't absorbing that possibility.

But he chuckled and rubbed her fingers, banishing the numbness from them. He pressed them against his chest, where she felt the unmistakable thumping of his heart.

"I am very much alive," Bastian informed her. "As are you."

"My lord...we have found shelter. Will is getting a fire started."

Bastian looked up at the man who spoke. "Excellent."

He stood and took her with him. A jolt of happiness went through her as she felt him cradling her against his chest.

Only Bastian had such strength.

Only her beast could carry her with ease.

"We're alive?" Alanna asked the question anyway.

Bastian looked down into her face. "Aye, we are."

Chapter Sixteen

ALANNA SAW THE sunrise.

She would have sworn she felt the first light of the day on her very skin. Even if such a thing were impossible, her eyes opened while the interior of the small house was still gray.

Yet the darkness was lightening.

Alanna smiled as she detected the hints of the day arriving. The shadows were being beaten back as the chill in the air began to recede.

Bastian was sleeping.

She lay for a moment, absorbing the sound of his breathing. She had to smother a little giggle as she thought about the fact that she was in bed with him…once more…and yet she was still a virgin.

There would be time for that later…

Laying there beside him was by far the most satisfying intimacy she had ever experienced. She had never felt so close to another soul. And yet, they knew so little about one another.

Time for that, too…

She eased from the bed, wanting to allow him to sleep. Someone had spread her dress out near the fire. Alanna happily put it on, eager to see the beginning of the day.

"Why are you in such a hurry?" Bastian asked from behind her.

Alanna turned to discover he'd left the bed without her hearing even a tiny rustle.

Of course…such was the Master of Stonebriar…

"You move so silently," she remarked.

His expression was guarded. "Are you leaving me, Alanna?"

The need to soothe the wrinkles from his forehead consumed her. She stepped toward him. "I didn't expect to see the sunrise ever again."

Understanding dawned in his eyes. His lips curved up into a genuine smile. "I suppose I understand your reasoning rather well myself."

He captured her hand. His larger one covering her smaller one completely. He lifted a finger and placed it on his lips to caution her to be quiet.

Once he led her out of the small room they'd slept in, Alanna understood why they needed to be quiet. In the next room, there were half a dozen men. They'd laid down on the floor to rest, the hoods of their sturdy surcoats pulled up to keep them warm.

Bastian went through them on silent steps as Alanna tried to keep her footfalls light. They made it to the door and outside without anyone moving.

Dawn was breaking.

Alanna smiled as she looked at the way the sunbeams were shining over the horizon. There were only a few white clouds in the sky, leaving nothing but blue as a backdrop for the sun.

"It's perfect," she exclaimed softly.

Bastian wrapped his arms around her. He tipped her chin up so that their gazes fused.

"Now it is perfect," he rasped out. "For you are in my arms, where you belong."

The doubts which had been lingering in her mind melted away under the warmth of his tone.

"Yes, I believe I agree completely with you."

She saw his eyes flicker with satisfaction a moment before he lowered his head and kissed her. The kiss was as warm as the rising sun. There wasn't an inch of her that wasn't heating while she mimicked his motions and kissed him back.

What good luck she had to have met him....

"ALANNA!" FIONA SPOTTED them first.

Her cousin came running across the yard. She caught Alanna up in a hug.

"I am so happy to see you!" Fiona squealed.

"So, the trollop's daughter has returned again," a new voice remarked.

"Your father's widow is here," Fiona remarked close to Alanna's ear.

Alanna faced her father's wife and performed a reverence. Lady Wydeville clicked her tongue and looked at Bastian.

"I must say," Lady Wydeville began, "You, sir, are quite the knave. I do not care for the way you trifle so openly with a member of my house."

"Bastian?" Her brother had appeared in the doorway.

"Really, Charles, I need to take this pair in hand before we have another bastard mouth to feed," Lady Wydeville muttered, her tone edged with disgust.

Her half-brother was trying to keep from smiling. "Mother...may I present Bastian Fulke, Lord Morely. One of his majesty's most trusted men."

The lady was not impressed. "As if that should ease my mind? Has he proposed marriage to your half-sister? Or is he once more dropping her on us to shelter and feed? Her reputation shredded."

"Forgive me, Lady Wydeville." Bastian clasped Charles' wrist in a greeting. "I am here to settle accounts with you."

"Settle...in what way?" Lady Wydeville demanded details.

For a moment, doubt needled Alanna because men of noble station could, and did, have lovers beyond the bonds of wedlock. The fact that she was still a maiden would never be believed.

Stop! He would do no such thing!...

Her confidence battled with her doubts and pushed them back.

"To your complete satisfaction," Bastian declared.

Lady Wydeville eyed him for a long moment before she smiled. She extended her hand so Bastian might kiss the back of it. "It is a pleasure to meet you, my lord."

THEY REACHED THE steps of Stonebriar just at sunset. Bastian slipped out of the saddle, coming back to help her dismount.

"Forgive me for not waiting," Bastian muttered. "Even if your lady stepmother was delighted to see us wed immediately. I imagine you would have liked to have a wedding."

"We had a wedding," Alanna insisted with a smile. "There were witnesses aplenty."

His lips twitched up as she smiled brightly at him. Alanna poked him in the chest with her finger.

"We are wed, Master of Stonebriar."

He performed a reverence, yielding to her in the matter. Once he straightened, he pointed at the stone tower.

"This is not my home. Now that my duty is complete, I will take you south tomorrow."

Alanna went forward and stood on the steps. "I believe it will always be a...special place for me."

Bastian raised an eyebrow as he came closer. "Those villagers were not wrong in choosing you for me."

"Is that so?" Alanna inquired as she took a step back.

"It most definitely is," Bastian assured her.

His expression charged, becoming one of passion. Alanna lingered for a moment to memorize it before she turned in a flare of skirts and ran. Bastian chased her up the steps, only catching her as she reached the chamber she considered hers now. He caught her close, sweeping her off her feet and carrying her toward their marriage bed.

The End

About the Author

Mary Wine has written over twenty novels that take her readers from the pages of history to the far reaches of space. Recent winner of a 2008 EPPIE Award for erotic western romance, her book LET ME LOVE YOU was quoted "Not to be missed..." by Lora Leigh, New York Times best-selling author.

When she's not abusing a laptop, she spends time with her sewing machines...all of them! Making historical garments is her second passion. From corsets and knickers to court dresses of Elizabeth I, the most expensive clothes she owns are hundreds of years out of date. She's also an active student of martial arts, having earned the rank of second degree black belt.

Printed in Great Britain
by Amazon

30834121R00046